# Singularity

# Singularity

Jayme A. Oliveira Filho and Jayme S. Alencar

ISBN:   978-1-63732-559-9   (Paperback Edition)
ISBN:   978-1-63732-560-5   (Hardcover Edition)
ISBN:   978-1-63732-558-2   (E-book Edition)

Some characters and events in this book are fictitious. Any similarity to real persons, living or dead, is coincidental and not intended by the author.

**Book Ordering Information**

Phone Number: 315 288-7939 ext. 1000 or 347-901-4920
Email: info@globalsummithouse.com
Global Summit House
www.globalsummithouse.com

Printed in the United States of America

# BOOK REVIEW

On a dying, late-21st-century Earth, a father and daughter discover transportation to distant space by means of black holes and seek to rescue a fragment of humanity via an evacuation ship.

This debut from a father-and-son writing team is a short SF novel about a multigenerational team of space scientists trying to save the human race—or what's left of it. Deep into the 21st century, global warming and overpopulation are clear signs that the Earth has little time left to support life. In the United States, Joseph Silva, a brilliant astrophysicist from a devout Christian Brazilian immigrant family, while watching his daughter, Daisy, has a brainstorm about black holes leading to other universes. Anything strong enough to travel through the "singularity" of the black hole can traverse the cosmos and potentially locate Earthlike habitats. Daisy grows up to be a scientist herself. She works at NASA on projects to confirm her father's theories and make his dream a reality: finding a new world to colonize before humanity perishes. The God-given gift of a meteorite laden with the unknown metal alloy "Munerium" enables construction of extremely strong space probes and ships to survive the black hole's gravity. Daisy gives birth to a son, Alexander, who will be instrumental to the planned mission through the singularity in 2135.

—KIRKUS REVIEWS

*Continue to page 73*

# CONTENTS

# DEDICATION

"THIS BOOK IS DEDICATED TO THE WOMAN, MEDICAL
DOCTOR, MOTHER, AND WIFE: CRISTINA ALENCAR"

TAS=LYA

# SUMMARY

The year 2020 has been a challenge for the whole mankind.

Wildfires, Storms, Drought, Death, Disease, COVID-19, Division, Violence, Social Injustice. This has been a tough year for all of us.

However, the night is darkest just before the Dawn.

SINGULARITY is a sci-fi book that focuses on the challenges that mankind will face during the 21st Century in special Global Warming. We will offer HOPE through human sacrifice, science, technology, faith, and imagination.

In the 1980s, scientists were warning us about the consequences of man-caused Global Warming and Climate Change. They warned us what could happen if we did not change our ways in the Future. Well, the FUTURE IS NOW. We are living the consequences of Global Warming.

We are breaking year after year the records for warmest year ever recorded. Droughts are more common, which cause more extensive and devastating wildfires throughout the world. Storms are becoming more constant and causing more damage. Ice caps are melting, which are causing more coastal floods.

THIS IS CLIMATE CHANGE AT WORK.

In our book, we will see the effects that Climate Change caused to the Earth's Population and what mankind had to do to save itself from extinction.

We will use science, physics, action, love, romance, sacrifice, faith, and religion to explain this Humankind journey throughout the 21st Century to the beginning of the 22nd Century.

I hope you enjoy our SCI-FI.
(www.jaymeandjayme.com)
GOD BLESS.

# CHAPTER ONE
## HOURGLASS

n the year 2135. Due to the indiscriminate use of natural resources and atmospheric pollution, the world is in disarray. Unscrupulous politicians of the 21$^{st}$ century did not believe the scientific community's warnings, and now the world is succumbing to its own greed. Wild climate with torrential storms, dust bowls, inundation, drought, oceans are rising, and coastal cities are disappearing. The world's population is in panic mode. States are crumbling as people are watching their lives come down to nothing. All hope is gone, the world is in dire need of a savior, but who is going to step out and raise its hand? What is it going to take to reverse all the damage that is lying around? The desperate cry of the world is unmistaken, yet the damage seems to be too big to even think of reversing what its inhabitants with a host of corrosive behaviors have been causing.

Nevertheless, like there is always an answer for everything happening under the sun —all mankind's hope rests on the shoulders of a young man and his crew as they try to find a new home. Alexander is an exceptionally talented young man, a natural leader, and a great recruit for the International Space Command Center (ISCC), where he met up with his love in an unusual environment. He uses science and his faith to become a wise leader. His family Motto is GOD'S BLESSINGS AND HARD WORK. He has this engraved on a bracelet given to him by his mother, Daisy.

Alexander always remembers their family motto and lives by this. He is also a devout Catholic Christian, just like his Great Grandparents that immigrated to the United States at the beginning of the 21st Century.

Alexander looks at a sandstorm forming over the horizon where before existed an exuberant forest. Holding the sand of the now desert, he remembers his great grandfather and the gift that could change the future of mankind.

Alexander's great grandparents were immigrants from Brazil. They came to the US to further their studies at the beginning of the 21$^{st}$ Century. His great grandmother was a medical doctor, and his great grandfather was a dentist. They just had one son —Joseph.

Joseph was very smart and an avid learner. He loved the Universe. When he was eight years old, he got a gift from his father that would change his life and possibly the future of the whole mankind.

Joseph got an Hourglass with the inscription: "Time is Relative. Brilliance is Not. From Darkness to Light". The beginning of the 21st Century was a period of many uncertainties in the world. Scientists were discussing the rapid increase of pollution in the atmosphere with the accumulation of $CO_2$. That build-up of Green House gases could cause the temperature to rise to the point of no return for the Earth. Scientists were giving their warnings, but politicians were not listening. It was in this context that Joseph received this gift from his dad, who was concerned about the future of the world, but it was also optimistic about the ingenuity of the human spirit.

Joseph grew up and realized his childhood dream and became an Astrophysicist, but he never forgot the gift that his dad gave to him and the inscription on it. By this time, the weather worldwide was becoming more unpredictable with longer droughts and stronger storms. In fact, he overhead some elderly people in a discussion that raised levels of interest in him. As he was passing by the old shop in his area, Joseph noticed that the elders were engaged in a tight conversation, judging by their intense engagement.

"It never used to be this long without the rains." One of them said before the other one, clad in an old, grey suit, "Yes, and we did not use to have a drought every two years. This is insane!"

Drought, huh? Joseph's curiosity was raised like that of a little child. So, indeed, his thoughts were right. It never used to drought as frequent as they are coming these years, something must have happened that caused all these shifts in the climate. Equally, something must also be done to right these wrongs from the past. Joseph was excited just thinking about this.

Nevertheless, he was trying to elaborate on a new theory about space and time. He had studied all the old and current concepts on Astronomy and Physics, but he was always fascinated about the beginning of everything. The Big Bang.

Thinking of the beginning of everything, it involves life, and everything around us —matter. And the Big Bang theory stated that the Universe started from the point of massive and unimaginable pressure and gravity, where all the matter in the Universe was concentrated into a point known as Singularity. He could never cope with the idea of everything coming from nothing. He was trying to devise a new theory that could explain that paradigm: "Everything Coming From Nothing."

And, looking at the above, we are drawn to the subject of Singularity in technology since the world today is vastly tech-driven. Looking at it from this angle, we notice that they define Singularity as "the hypothesis that the invention of artificial superintelligence will abruptly trigger huge technological growth, resulting in unfathomable changes to human civilization." These changes obviously speak of many creations that are to come out of this intelligence. As such, besides speaking of a Big Bang that could have resulted in the creation of the universe including its many features and life that is in it, we could be talking of a tech-driven Big Bang —with humans at the center of it all —resulting in creations that benefit humans at large.

However, Joseph was a brilliant young man, recognized by his expertise and wit. He was immensely proud of his Brazilian-American heritage, and he wanted to make his Silva family proud of him. He was also a big fan of Albert Einstein, which had revolutionized science at the beginning of the 20$^{th}$ Century with his Relativity Theory and many thought experiments. Einstein also created the idea that the universe is not just an empty space, but everything is correlated and interconnected through a medium that he called the "Space-Time Fabric." With this new concept, Einstein explained that Gravity is the interaction of mass distorting this fabric around them. This distortion is what creates the orbits, just like the gravity wells in Science museums. When you throw a coin inside the well, the coin follows the curvature of the well until it falls inside of it. Those wells are a particularly good representation of the distortion that objects with a big mass cause in this Space-Time fabric, and that distortion promotes the movement of objects around them, like the planets around the sun. His theory was proven in 2016 when gravitational waves were first detected.

Joseph loved thought experiments and the concept of the Space-Time Fabric established by Einstein. He liked to imagine situations in his head to solve difficult problems. It was in one of his thought experiments that he would create a new theory that could revolutionize the science world and could reshape the future of Astrophysics.

Besides being an Astrophysicist, Joseph was also a father of a young girl named Daisy. One day, he took Daisy to a park, and she went to jump on a trampoline. He started to see his lovely daughter jumping in this trampoline, going higher and higher, but he also observed that the trampoline fabric was being distorted when she was landing on it.

His mind went wild in one of his thought experiments. What if his daughter kept jumping in the trampoline until she would stretch to a point in which she could not be stretched no longer? What would happen? An ordinary mind would say she is going to fall to the ground. However, Joseph did not have an ordinary mind. His mind was wildly imaginative. Therefore, he imagined that his daughter would keep distorting the fabric until a point that she would move to another place, another dimension, another universe. He started thinking. What could do that in the universe? What was so massive that could distort the fabric of the Space-Time to a point of collapse, and he thought: A Black Hole.

A black hole is a point of extreme gravity in the universe that not even light can escape from his immense pull. But at that time the concept it was that a Black Hole would squeeze all the matter that enter it into a point called Singularity.

So, Joseph thought: The Big Bang started with a Singularity and the Black Hole ends in a Singularity, what could possibly be the connection of both? And then he remembered the gift that his father had given to him when he was eight years old. The Hourglass with the inscription: "From Darkness to Light." What if, "Nothing" actually came from "Something"? What if like an Hourglass, matter flowed from one space to the other? What if a huge Black hole would distort and disrupt the fabric of Space-Time to the point of Rupture? All the matter being absorbed by that Black Hole would be transferred to another universe through a Big Bang. "From Darkness to Light," "From Black Hole to a Big Bang."

In a single instant, his mind was open to the vastness of the universe. He was floating in the middle of the Milky Way Galaxy, looking straight to the monster Black Hole called Sagittarius A Star. He was going inside to the Singularity of the black hole, through a tunnel being funneled to another Singularity, a Wormhole to a brand new Big Bang Universe. He could see everything so clearly on his mind. The Cosmos became a Multiverse with many Universes interacting with each other by destruction and creation. "From Darkness to Light."

When he came back from his thought experiment, which seemed like an eternity to him, Daisy was still jumping on the trampoline. She had no idea what had just happened and the part that she would play in the future to help prove his father's theory right.

"Dad?" She looked at him, obviously looking tired and wanted to go back home. But she did not say the words because her dad looked like he was caught up in his own galaxy. And he was surely kept up on his own.

"Oh, yes, you want to go back home, I guess?" He asked her as he was getting ready to go. "Yes, daddy, I think I have had enough for today. I am tired.

"Mm. I like that!" He looked towards her direction, showing off somewhat brown teeth as he grinned. "So, you like it when I am tired?" She asked him back, of which he responded, "No, sweetheart, when you are tired, it means that you have been exercising, and exercising is always good for your body. It stays fit, and you sleep well".

"Whatever!" She smiled back at him. Joseph smiled at her too, but still, his whole mind was still caught up in what he could do in his science project. We understand him because, for everything that gets created in this world, the creator goes through enormous thinking time, with many things being cooked in his mind before laying things on the ground.

This is a reminder about what one friend told us what happens when we asked about his car making career. So, he said that everything is designed in the mind of the designer, after which they do come up with a design, which they put down to paper. In this design, all the mechanics and measurements will be rightly written down, of course, using a standard scale from the company—just like what folks who are into geology do when they measure a whole country's perimeter using a scale of a centimeter to represent a certain number of kilometers.

Nevertheless, we are saying that all things are prepared for in mind—but the most important thing is the fact that, after they have been cooked up in mind, they must be comprehensively laid down on paper for both the originator and his audience or future originators to study this original creation.

So, Joseph's battle was for him to complete the puzzle in his mind. But in science, sometimes the puzzle is completed after long trials on paper. Rather than bringing the creation or equation straight to paper, already completed, it may take time, writing it down one, two, or more times before deleting some variables and adding some until everything is brought to the right order.

The journey back home seemed noticeably short for both Joseph and his daughter. They did have their own trampoline in their backyard, but I guess they need the special father-daughter moment away from home. Even though it was for achieving that, the short walk to the community park resulted in the birth of a special idea in Joseph's mind. So, aside from the fact that his daughter was ecstatic, he was over the moon too, and some of his smiles were not because his daughter was happy that they had gone out, but it was also because of the things that kept on coming to his mind, especially because they were conceived after watching his daughter go up and down using the pressure that she applied on the trampoline each time she descended on it.

# CHAPTER TWO
## THE IMPACT

So, previously, we spoke about Joseph coming back from the playground with his daughter. Their little time out gave birth to an exciting idea, and now he was all ready to explore it, quietly.

Therefore, he started working on his theory. He had a big question that he had to answer. What if our universe is inside a black hole and the dark energy that continues to expand our universe is matter being constantly absorbed by this black hole from another universe? Therefore, the singularity of the above-mentioned black hole would be the singularity of our Big-Bang. Both singularities would be connected by a wormhole.

This concept of expanding Universe was proven and established by famous 20th Century astronomer Edwin Hubble that through his observations and calculations in 1929, postulated that the Universe was not static, but in fact. expanding. And more recent calculations have shown that this rate of expansion is accelerating.

For readers who have no strong background on the subject, a wormhole can be defined as the solutions to the Einstein field equations for gravity. It is what acts the same way as "tunnels" that are responsible for connecting the points in space-time. During the process, it will be done in such a way that taking the trip between the points (between the Earth and, perhaps, Mars) through the wormhole could take much less time than the trip through normal space. However, we will talk about the time it takes, according to what we are writing about in this book.

Going back to the expansion of the Universe concept, it would be almost like someone blowing a balloon constantly. This balloon would get bigger and bigger and bigger, and because the balloon would be constantly being blown; therefore, it would constantly be getting bigger. The rate of expansion would be the rate of the balloon being blown. The balloon would continue to grow indefinitely because it is being blown indefinitely until no more air/matter is available to be put inside the balloon/universe.

So, Joseph developed his mathematical formulas. And they were as follows:

Expansion Rate = Velocity Rate of Matter being sucked by the black hole. (ER = BHMv).

Black hole matter = visible matter + dark matter + dark energy. (BHM=VM+DM+DE).

Black Hole & Big Bang (B.H. & B.B.)

If we could calculate how big it had to be – the black hole that would create our universe, thereby being the one to solve the equation {Black Hole size = Space/Time (13.7billion years) + visible matter + dark matter + dark energy} [BHs=S/T+VM+DM+DE].

That would also solve the question of whether the information is lost inside a black hole. In fact, information is not lost. It is just transferred to another universe. Per Lavoisier, in nature, nothing is lost, and everything is transformed, from chemical elements to entire Universes. In this light, a new black hole would create a new universe and transform matter into a new Big Bang. Is that crazy? He thought. Am I going to be able to prove that? This is what is called the Multiverse Theory. That there are infinite Universes in our Cosmos.

Indeed, proving things is the difficult part about it, especially when figuring out how you are going to translate what is in your mind to the paper, and eventually to the people. The process must be seamless, and most importantly, people respond well to what has been scientifically proven before. If not, know that the task is going to be insurmountable by the time we get to face the world to let it know what we are on about. In a way, Joseph was at the beginning of such a mission and was intending to win in all possible ways. The motivation was good, and so was the logic behind his 'creation,' or soon to be.

Nevertheless, it, indeed, was not easy for him. He was ridiculed and ostracized from the same institutions that one day applauded him for his achievements in astrophysics. The battle took a long time raging on, but he had a determination that was never seen before. To see just how it took, he went on that trip with his daughter when she was only eight when she played on the trampoline, but the battle raged on until she was actually old enough to understand what was going on —and be inspired by her dad.

Her dad was a truly inspired man because he devoted his life into trying to prove his theory. Like we have mentioned before, his work was not going unnoticed, especially by some people closer to him, including his daughter. He influenced his beloved daughter, Daisy, in a special way. She saw how passionate her father was about the Universe and the work that he put into everything that came with it. As such, she decided to become an Aerospace Engineer for NASA as soon as she was old and qualified enough.

She always tried to help her dad in finding the proof for his theory, but she became sad to see his father's former friends making fun of him and his theory. At some point, it would get very ugly with his friends saying all sorts of mean things to him. These are some of the things that happen in life —when things seemingly do not work in your favor. Some friends mock you, while some even go ahead and desert you. They will call you all sorts of names but what is important is to always know that you got a dream that requires your protection. For Joseph, it was very difficult because for every man, you can imagine how embarrassing it is for people that are close to you to be mocking you in front of your wife and kids. In order to ignore all their hateful words, it took a man that understood what he wanted to achieve, and his heart was very convinced that it is going to work one day.

It is such a level of courage that drew Daisy into liking her dad and the work that he did. In fact, it makes so much sense because Daisy always lived close to her dad. They were so close, so much so that she saw his every step. She was even there when the dream was born, back when she was eight. It reminds us of the fact that sometimes friends and associates mock us the most because they think they have the full knowledge of the things that we do. However, it is not true because some of the things happen deep in our closets when everyone else is not around. And it happened like that for Joseph.

So, Daisy would speak to her dad in her sweet little voice, you can imagine her head tilted to one side because of the concern. She would always ask her dad why he continued to pursue his theory against so many detractors. He would tell her: "Never let anyone tell you what you have to do. If you believe in something, fight for it to the end". He would also tell her: "One day I will be proved right. I believe in this. I will keep trying and practicing my theory because you know…" and she would answer: "Practice Makes It Perfect." That was a saying that her father would always tell her when something would not go right. Keep trying, keep practicing, one day you shall overcome.

But in this case, the practicing part was taking long enough. A kid would be born and complete primary education, and it was still being perfected. It is like that in life. There are so many interesting stories, especially in the technological world, that were born of similar situations. People would toil for a long time just trying to fix one equation so that when the product is finally out, it will make so much sense. But sometimes when they think it is almost over, for example, those dealing in Information Technology, sometimes you hear them say that we do have to improve a certain 'security patch' or something like that. Indeed, Joseph's work was so big that it had to take such time. Imagine you are Elon Musk, and you invented a self-driving car only to realize that your security patching is weak, and the next thing you hear that hackers are having access to your self-driving cars and leading to all sorts of accidents?

So, by the time that bad friends and detractors are saying all sorts of bad things, the inventor, in this case, Joseph, will be fully aware of the extent of the work that he is doing and how important or groundbreaking it is going to be. Such work must be carefully planned and expertly executed. Failure of which leads to a monumental failure and a story that people will never forget. He just did not want to be in the books of history for the wrong reasons, even when he was gone. Luckily, his daughter was in full support of him—it made it sweet like icing on the cake even as the dream was taking time to be realized.

So, Daisy believed in her dad and vowed to help him prove his theory right. Therefore, she began to actively involve herself in the whole process. She did this because sometimes just sending a solidarity message alone is not enough. It will just be like politicians who say we support you with your idea with completely nothing to back up their message. So, for Daisy, the only way to support her dad's dream would be to send a probe inside a black hole and collect the DATA from inside of it. That was an impossible task at the time. First, Sagittarius A was thousands of light-years away, in the middle of the Milky Way Galaxy. To be more precise, 26,000 light-years (a lightyear is the time that light takes to travel for one year from one object to the other). Second, they would need a computer capable of sending information from inside the black hole. Third, no probe would be able to enter a black hole without being destroyed by the immense gravity inside of it.

This just made things seem more difficult. But it is what it is in life. I can tell that the best of us have come across some serious challenges when on a mission to achieving something great for both ourselves and the people around us. More so, this was not just some small mission, but it was something so great that it would naturally attract some hard tasks going ahead. But, as we have mentioned that the motivation was there, it would come to pass, just one day.

Therefore, Daisy knew this, and she started working in her specialty. She started developing a probe capable to travel to a black hole and survive the gravity of it. She started trying a plethora of metal alloys trying to find the right combination to support the immense gravity, but all samples would fail during tests. Every time that she was getting frustrated, Daisy would remember her father saying: "Practice Makes It Perfect." and she would continue the tests.

As for Joseph, he was getting old, and Daisy was afraid that her dad would never see his theory being proved right. She had the design and concept for the probe, but she could not solve the three problems, Distance, Information, and Resistance. But that all changed in a morning of 2071.

A meteor was supposed to strike Earth in the Sahara Desert. Scientists waited for the impact, and as usual, they started studying the meteor, but this was no ordinary meteor. The impact crater was immense, and the meteor was not fragmented as they expected. The meteor remained intact, even with a huge impact. Analyzing the rock, they observed that it was almost completed composed of a metal alloy never seen before. Scientists held a press conference to release the discovery to the scientific community and the public. They called this new metal alloy: Munerium. Daisy was at her house, having her breakfast when she glanced on the TV to see an ongoing news conference. She immediately thought that the meteor could be the missing piece for her probe. If the meteor was capable of being intact after such an unbelievable collision, maybe the metal alloy would be strong enough to support the immense gravity of a black hole.

She contacted the scientists that had analyzed the rock and asked for a sample for studies. They were reluctant at the beginning. However she pushed forward and contacted her NASA friends, and they could get a sample to her.

She started studying the alloy, and she could not believe it. The alloy could withstand the tests of enormous gravitational pressure. "Eureka!", she exclaimed. "I found my missing piece!" Now she would need help to solve the other two questions of the puzzle and sooner than she thought, she would get that help.

# CHAPTER THREE
## SPACE JUMP

n 2074, two scientists were in a friendly competition to see which one would have the biggest development of the Decade. Professor Christine was developing the first Quantum Computer. This computer was in the works for decades, but she was almost decoding the last details to make it fully operational.

Yes, it was in development for decades, unbelievable, right? But like we mentioned in the previous chapter, these kinds of developments take ample time to bring to completion. No one really wants to produce something that takes that amount of knowledge and time only for it to falter in the end. This is the same thing as what happened in the previous chapter with Joseph and Daisy. They were patient enough to wait for the right moment before seeing the dream in action. Joseph had to wait until a time when his daughter was getting scared that he could age and die without seeing his dream come to life. So, looking at this, the years that it took for Professor Christine's Quantum Computer are justified.

Nevertheless, Quantum Computers (QC) are based on the theory of Quantum Physics and Quantum Mechanics. They use the property known as quantum entanglement, which states that when two objects or particles are in contact, they remain connected forever and does not matter how far apart they are. That would make it possible to have an instant connection and information between unimaginable points in the Universe or different Universes.

No matter how far apart they are? I can feel some heads being turned, especially on people that have no strong background in physics or sciences. Well, for starters, we would like to say that quantum entanglement brings forth a deeper understanding of the several worlds of the quantum theory. Remember, we learned that Joseph was dreaming of proving what it would take for the Earth to finally be moved to Mars, in a Big Bang fashion. It explains the two worlds that could be brought together via a wormhole.

So, going back to the issue of quantum entanglement, we understand that the quantum theory requires multiple worlds for it to exist or function. And, when there is quantum entanglement, we will have two worlds that are not independent of each other. With this, what do we mean? Well, we may use the two worlds that we know best these days because of what has been happening in the USA and China and the rest of the advanced world. If you are into science and the exploration of the worlds away from us, the Earth, you will know that we are speaking about the exploration of Mars that has been discussed extensively in the past few months, with also private organizations getting into the fold and trying to commercialize the whole thing.

Nonetheless, without getting carried away, when we speak of quantum entanglement, we speak of the two worlds that are not much independent from each other, and these could be the Earth and Mars. Well, we said we picked Mars because it's been so much of a topic in the past few months, and we also picked the Earth because we live in it —even though human activity and climate change are doing so much damage to it by each passing year. These worlds are said to not be independent of each other because the more you are knowledgeable about one, the more you get to know the other. For example, if the relationship between the earth and mars is like that, then if we, by chance, discover that the earth is actually a hexagon, then we will definitely know that Mars is also a hexagon in shape. Once again, these are just examples that we are giving. They could be shaped like an oval. It doesn't matter. But here, what matters is if we can link their relationship positively —or something they call positive correlation in statistics.

Moving on, we do have Professor Heart, who was developing a new type of propulsion called Ionic Nuclear Graviton Engine (INGE). This new propulsion system would be able, in theory, to distort the space-time fabric around a spaceship and create a Wormhole, a short cut through space-time. Per his calculations, he could decrease a travel of 1,000 light-years to more or less an Earth Hour for the occupants of the Spaceship, and that would represent one year for the Earth's population. As Einstein proposed in the past, Time is Relative. A person flying in space has a different time count and perspective than someone on Earth. This is due to Gravity and his General Relativity Theory.

Gravity, once again for those not so much versed in science, is an important phenomenon that represents the fact that everything with mass or energy with it will be pulled together or brought towards one another. When you jump, it is gravity that takes you down to the earth. As such, gravity gives us and other objectives weight. In space, as humans were to go there, just like what happens to ashes when you toss them into the air —they take time just flying around above the surface because they do not have meaningful weight in them. So, we are saying that, because of this gravity, a person traveling in space experiences a different time count than when they are on earth. This is because TIME IS RELATIVE. The perception of time depends upon the observer.

So, Professor Heart had an amazingly simple explanation for his theory. Imagine a sheet of paper, and on that sheet of paper, you have a point in each extremity. Regular physics says that the smaller distance between two points is a straight line, but if you could bend the paper in half, one could make the two points contact. That was the whole principle behind his idea. Create a short cut between two points in space by creating a wormhole. He called his concept Space Jump.

Both were brilliant scientists, and they were running against time.

You could be wondering why all this need for these scientists to create a connection between the two worlds. Well, we mentioned earlier before just how the Earth is being ravished by climate change. And because of it, coupled with human activity, the Earth has seen a great deal of damage. Resources are dwindling at an even faster rate such that it will come a time when it is difficult to allocate resources that are enough for every person efficiently. Even Economists with their theories on allocating scarce resources would struggle. Therefore, this is the justification that we can give to the scientists that are busy looking for a breakthrough into another world that is not the Earth.

As such, we notice that bit this time, when our good professors are busy with their inventions, and in 2074, the weather on Earth had reached a tipping point because of extreme human activity such as deforestation and farming or construction on wetlands, among many other things. Even the skeptics started to believe that something was not right with our planet. Coastal cities were being flooded, droughts were becoming more severe, storms had become stronger than ever, crises were being triggered in many countries, and millions were dying every year from the effects of Climate Change. Scholars were not optimistic about the future of mankind on Earth because the Weather patterns have achieved a case of Positive Feedback in a vicious cycle that year after year, the weather was becoming more and more hostile to the world population. Everyone was looking for the skies to look for a possible livable planet or moon to sustain Earth's population. This is what is called the Runaway Greenhouse Effect. This same process happened to Earth's twin, Venus, Billions of years ago. This effect destroyed the planet's atmosphere, and it became unbearable for life. The temperature on Venus's surface is hotter than Mercury's, due to the heat being trapped by the Greenhouses in Venus's atmosphere. In Venus, the culprit for this calamity was the Volcanoes, while on Earth it is the human activity with the release of $CO_2$ in the atmosphere.

The extent of the damage was massive. We saw even the biggest optimists who always said things would be alright giving up on life and always living life expecting the worst to happen at any time. In terms of probability, the children that were being born those days were being given extraordinarily little chances that they would survive and live longer until they are old enough to hold their grandchildren in their hands.

Therefore, it was immensely important to have both Professor Christine and Professor Heart's concepts proven to start looking for a suitable location for human colonization. And a glimmer of hope sparkled when both Professors announced that they had finished their products and were ready to be tested, but they need a spaceship strong enough to support the astronomical gravitational fluctuations involved in this experiment.

Even though the news had brought a glimmer of hope to the people, the fact that there was still something amiss meant that the smiles faded back to sorrow in an instant. All those people wanted to hear was the fact that the professors' work was ready to be used. You can imagine the anxiety that was already there — whether the professors' products were going to work or not and the fact that they needed to find something else for transporting their work—a spaceship which they did not have.

Nevertheless, it did not take much time before people's hopes were brought back up again. This time, it was the fact that the two professors had contacted Daisy. They had heard about her experiments with Munerium and her development of a space probe with it. Daisy was ecstatic to hear about it. Finally, she would be able to test Joseph's theory about black holes and new universes, but the Professors had other ideas. They told her that they would not send the probe to Sagittarius A Star. They just wanted to test the concepts of Space Jump and the Quantum Computer to see if they would work. Daisy was adamant that she would just use her probe if, after the first test, they allow her to test her dad's hypothesis about other Universes.

You see, this is how it should be in life —for people to embrace the power of negotiation. We just thought about it and thought, why not say this to the people. After all, life revolves around using what you have at your disposal as ammunition to get more of the things you wish for —it is more like a continuous trade of skills and possessions. Nevertheless, as these scientists were doing it for the benefit of the people, you must also know that selfish ambitions must not have a place in society, especially with the way climate change is completely ravaging the world. It will take a united effort to end it. And now we have three people in a team of one —Daisy and the two professors.

Nevertheless, enough about the motivation on love. Going back to Daisy and the professors, they reached a compromise in the end, and it was for the wellbeing of mankind, just like we have already alluded to. Because they had an agreement in place, the Trifecta was finally assembled. Engine-Computer-Probe were ready for launch —what a day for the hopeful masses as well as the scientists that were ready to start something to save the world from the deteriorating climate and all the bad things that came with it.

They decided that the first test would be in a relatively empty area of the Milky Way Galaxy 1,000 light/years away from Earth. That would take the probe about one hour in Space-Time but would take one year in Earth time. If that test was successful, they would send probes to Sagittarius A Star.

A date was set for the test, and on September the 22$^{nd}$, 2075, a Rocket left the Earth, carrying the probe out of space. And from there, the rocket released the probe, and the Ionic Nuclear Graviton Engine was fired, and the Quantum Computer started running. The probe created a distortion in the Space-Time fabric to form a Wormhole, which was successfully formed.

Now, they could just wait to see if the Quantum Computer receiver on mission control would receive any information from the probe. And wait, they did.

The time finally came to get the first information from the probe. If the calculations were correct, Professor Christine said, "We should get data from the probe on the next hours". It had been a year since the launch, and everyone was very anxious.

They waited, waited, and hours became days and days became a week. Professors Christine and Heart were dismayed. What might have happened? Maybe the probe was not strong enough, or maybe the quantum computer did not work, or maybe the Space Jump was unsuccessful, but Daisy didn't miss a bit. She kept telling them that it will work. "I know it will." She had developed the patience from the years that she waited to develop her father's idea —from the time that she was a young girl to the time that she grew up to become an adult. So, if the people needed to be patient at the time, there was no one else fully qualified to help with that than her.

Just as how it is with all the good news that is waited upon, the news, or data finally arrived! On day 9 of the waiting period, the Quantum Computer sent a signal that said that the ship had reached the destination, and all the instruments were working in well and in perfect condition. The Mission Control exploded in celebration upon seeing that. They pulled it off —they had pulled the almost impossible.

Professors Christine and Heart could not contain themselves, but Daisy was incredibly quiet. She was happy, but she was not yet satisfied. She was thinking about Joseph and everything that he had to endure since he told the world his theory about Black Holes and the Big Bang. Now, she had the chance to prove her dad was right, and she would not let that chance go away.

# CHAPTER FOUR
## INTO THE DARKNESS

**M**unerium was material that came in an asteroid that impacted on Earth. It was an extraordinary material that had the fantastic quality to get even stronger when submitted to immense PRESSURE and Gravity. You know, just like that boy in school who would perform very well when under pressure. Indeed, we used to have such friends, and they would wait for the exam time to come for them to begin preparing, yet others would have been on it for an exceedingly long time. However, even if they would wait until the end of the semester to study in their numbers, these guys would do it in different ways. For some, they would engage in activities that trained their memories to grasp concepts for a short space of time, just so they can go through the exam and forget about it, but others would do it to remember what they write in the exams forever.

In the same manner, we could describe how the Munerium adapted to pressure and outperformed. It also did it in a quite different way, unique to itself. This reminds us of how people define particles in quantum physics using their behavior. Therefore, the behavior of the Munerium also led to people defining it the way they did. So, the atoms that formed the material would transform to a crystalline structure practically indestructible when tested under infinite pressure and gravity —there we go, this is how it did it.

It was a miracle material that came from Space/Heavens to give hope and save MANKIND. We know for some, this could come hard to fathom, but for believers in science, this was truly a gift as we would see how this helped to bring a cause to fruition.

The Munerium asteroid fell in the middle of the Sahara Desert, and it created a huge crater, but the most dramatic fact about the impact is that THE ASTEROID was intact. It did not break a single piece. Since a long time ago, people knew that wherever an asteroid fell from the sky, it would break into several fragments because of the impact it would have made with the Earth. If we were to measure the weight that an average asteroid has while falling from the sky, you would be surprised by what we find out. And, given the fact that it was falling from the sky, this added more weight to it because of gravity. But still, with all the weight, it did not even break a little.

The story of Munerium was, indeed, a miracle. As people were busy wondering what kind of an asteroid this could be, they came up with an idea to call Daisy so that she could study this stone. They were optimistic that something would come out of it. To be fair, we believe that optimism is what brings people to the birth of many great ideas that help the world run smoothly. Some of the tasks that people embark on are just enormous, and without optimism, it would be difficult to cut through it even to the halfway line. But Daisy came from a background that did not lack optimism, especially when looking at the life of her father and his aspirations that he did not give up on even when he watched himself grow old before proving his theory.

"Daisy, there is someone on the line for you." That was Marlene, Daisy's assistant, talking to her boss after receiving a call from the people that needed help. It was a simple phone call that completely changed her next few days as she went on a new discovery —a life that she had devoted herself to because of how she used to watch her dad when growing up.

As alluded to, after answering the call, she agreed to this new mission, especially after speaking to her assistant, who had asked her what it was about because she had seen an unusual reaction on Daisy's face as she responded to the call. But even though the reaction was unusual, she managed to speak to Marlene in a way that drew assurances from her.

So, she went on to this mission, and eventually, Marlene was the one that made the connection between the oxygen isotope inside Munerium and the one on the Moon. While making the connection, she also explained to them what this means, especially looking at how the Muneirum resisted breaking into small fragments after the huge impact that it made when falling on earth. This discovery was really important because, in order to fabricate the huge amounts of Munerium necessary to build a giant spaceship, we would need to create synthetic Munerium somewhere, and because of this characteristic of the oxygen isotope, that place had to be the Moon. This would be the catalyst for the construction of the Lunar Base.

After making the connection between the oxygen isotope inside Munerium and the one on the Moon, Daisy had an idea that was going to help send the ship into the black hole for information without it being torn apart because of the immense gravitational pressure inside the black hole. Eventually, there was going to be a way to send a ship into the "dark space" and obtain the information that was required. Daisy had been tasked to make sure that the ships to be sent there were strong enough to resist Spaghettification, which is a process whereby there are immense vertical stretching and horizontal compression of objects into long thin shapes that are like spaghetti, in a very strong non-homogeneous gravitational field. This is caused by extreme tidal forces, and that happens when any matter enters the Black Hole.

So, because there was now enough knowledge to make sure that the probes to be sent into the black hole would not break, scientists involved were thrilled to be able to now anticipate their first mission. How would this really work? So, with the probes and the ship, Knight Discoverer, what will happen is that it will contract and condense the atoms that the volume will decrease by 50%, and the length will be stretched to 4 times the original length. And, with it being stretched this hard, there was the fear that anything else would break and throw their work of years into the air, but now there was something else that was usable. It became possible because Munerium is the only substance known in the Universe capable of resisting the immense pressure and gravity of a black hole.

As such, it was now time to design the probes and the ship. All the information was gathered, and this new discovery, through the Munerium, was going to play an important role. More so, the probes and the ship were now destined to be designed in a way that they are very sleek and wider rather than taller. Doing it this way would give them more chances of surviving the pressure inside the black hole because it is known for consuming or sending away everything that comes near it because of its very strong gravitational pull.

# CHAPTER FIVE
## BITTERSWEET

D aisy designed two probes that would be sent to the Black Hole in the middle of the Milky Way Galaxy, Sagittarius A Star. She named the probes Allen and Carr. Both probes were fabricated with the remaining Munerium obtained from the meteor that stroke the Sahara Desert. Each probe also contained 200 space drones designed to search the new Universe in case Joseph's theory was corrected. These drones were equipped with an Ionic Engine and Quantum computer.

Allen and Carr were taken to orbit with a conventional rocket. From there, they were released into space, and the Ionic Engine was turned on, and the Quantum computer was also turned on.

The journey should take 26 hours for the probes, but for people on Earth, it would take 26 years for them to know if the probes made through their journey and survived their encounter with the Black Hole. This is due to the Relativity of Time. As we already discussed before, according to Einstein's General Relativity Theory, time is relative and perceived as such depending on the influence of gravity and speed.

Now the waiting game would start. They would have to wait for 26 years to see if Joseph's theory was correct or not. Daisy was worried if her dad would still be alive to see the conclusion of this chapter on their lives.

The Space Control Center was a lonely place for Daisy. She could just wait.

After 13 years of the probes' launch, Daisy got a call in the middle of the night from her Assistant Marlene.

Marlene said, "Daisy, you need to come to the Space Control Center."

Daisy asked, "What happened?"

Marlene replied, "Allen just started transmitting DATA."

Daisy said, "That is impossible! The probes could not transmit DATA inside the Wormhole unless it came out."

And that is exactly what happened. Allen Ionic Engine failed middle way through its Journey and stopped in the middle of the Milky Way Galaxy. The Quantum Computer started transmitting info, and they detected a problem with the engine ventilation system that made it overheat and stop working. That is the reason why the probe stopped and was lost in the middle of the Galaxy.

All the hope now rested on Carr's shoulders to see if it would survive the journey and the encounter with Sagittarius A Star.

They would have to wait another 13 years to know that. Meanwhile, they were analyzing info being transmitted by Allen and the details from the Engine that quit mid-way.

After long 26 years, Carr was just about to enter the Massive Black Hole in the middle of the Galaxy, and it was time to see if it would start transmitting what was programmed to come out of the wormhole. The air was tense inside Space Control Center. The anxiety was palpable, and Daisy could barcly control herself. They started to wait for any signal from the probe. And they waited, waited, and waited, and when they were about to call it a day, the probe started transmitting. The Control room exploded in celebration. Carr had survived the journey, and it was about to plunge inside the Black Hole. According to Daisy's calculations, the probe should suffer the spaghettification process with compression to about 50% of its volume and a stretch of 4 times its length. Hopefully, her calculations were right, and the probe would survive the unimaginable gravity of the Black Hole.

The probe went inside the black hole and again stopped transmitting info. This should be quick. One way or the other, they should have an answer today if the probe was destroyed or if the probe survived, and it had gone through the Singularity of the Black hole to the Singularity of a new Universe. They waited for hours and days. Daisy was destroyed. She thought everything was lost, and she could no longer prove her dad's theory. But something inside her told her to go to the Space Center that Sunday morning to check the monitors. She got there, and an indication light was blinking in one of the Monitors. She could not believe what she was seeing. Carr was transmitting. Carr was sending info from a NEW UNIVERSE. She could not contain her emotion and started crying. She started thinking, Dad was right all this time. He was right.

Daisy started running diagnostics on the probe. It had survived, but it was damaged on its journey through the Black Hole. Just half of the space drones were available and operational for deployment and exploration of this New Universe. This was important because these drones would start searching this new Universe for a habitable planet for humans. This was a mission to prove her dad's theory, but also to look for a new home for mankind. Earth was dying, and we would need to find a new home. The space probes were sent away.

After working with Professor Christine and Professor Heart, one can only imagine the joy that filled Daisy's heart. This was to be one of the days that she rejoiced that, after many years of working hard, trying to prove her father's theory, she eventually had found the answers. Remember when she was young, bouncing her beautiful body on that trampoline, that was the moment when the dream was born in her father's mind. But until this day, when both of them were now older, it was yet to be proven.

Imagine the kind of joy that she had when she went to visit her father. But even when she was this happy, something else was not all too well in their family. When she got there, she found Joseph lying still on his death bed when she went to see him and give the good news that one of the probes had survived the journey, and it had proven his theory that on the other side of a black hole lies a new universe.

For her, the survival of one of the probes and the coming of the good news was worth celebrating. But seeing her dad lying in that death bed was not the scene that she was expecting nor anticipating. You could see the tears forming in her eyes as she spoke to him. Those tears were not just because of the exhilaration of their achievement, but also because of seeing her dad lying in that bed. This was the man that she used to know running around, spending the better part of the night with inexplicable energy just working to prove his theory.

I am sure that many kids can attest to this. It is not easy watching your parent growing old and not being able to do anything for themselves, and the sight is even more painful to see when it was the parent that used to do everything by themselves and could self-sustain for their entire lives. What makes it more painful is that, by them being used to doing things for themselves, old age and sickness can drive them into inability for their remaining time on Earth, which drives their minds crazy. It is like that even when the body is no longer able to sustain difficult tasks. Their minds will still be in for it, thinking that they can still do it. But, as soon as they try to lift their finger, feel that it is impossible to do anything —which drives them to sadness.

So, you can imagine what was going through his mind hearing that his child had finally made it? Was he thrilled of the results, or it even reminded him that he is now an old man just waiting to die?

Nevertheless, Daisy and her dad both cried because they knew this was the last conversation they would have. Even when they were bound to be celebrating, Joseph was still facing death, and that on its own is scary. But for him, it was also a blessing to finally hear that his theory has been proven to be true.

Daisy said to her dying dad, "You were RIGHT, Papa. All this time, you were right. You made the biggest discovery of the Century. This is the greatest achievement of ALL time!" She looked desperate for her dad to understand that he had made it, even though he was no longer involved in the last stages of proving the theory. She had her eyes wide open, almost wearing an innocent look of a child, just trying to make sure that her dad understands that even if he dies, his work would be remembered forever.

Almost without any more voice, he mustered these words, "You, my beloved daughter, was my greatest achievement. What you became will be my legacy." Clearly, talking was now something difficult for him as he struggled to continue talking to his daughter. When he said she was her achievement, it almost seemed as if he was giving up on all his achievements because he was not there when it all yielded the results. Daisy sensed it and reminded him that had it not been for his initial work all those years back, nothing of this sort would have been achieved. She also told him that whatever work that she would end up doing later in her life, it was all because of Joseph's ideas and work. So, even if he wanted to pin all the success on Daisy, it was his to relish.

After Daisy's speech about how this was all his work, she was delighted to see that smile back on his father's face. Even though it was difficult to bring it on, it came out, and she knew that he finally understood just how he had worked very hard for this, and it was all because of his mind that this day was made possible. As for Joseph, he looked sideways as the smile on his face broke into that concerned countenance. He knew that his time had come. He struggled to look his daughter in the face knowing that in a few minutes, their celebration will be turned into mourning.

Nevertheless, he was a soldier in his heart. He turned his face back to her and said, "Please take the Hourglass and this necklace with the crucifix on it." As soon as he asked for those things, Daisy knew that the time had come, and she felt cold in her heart. For a moment, it was like the world around her was spinning. She did not even see when he took his last breath. As soon as she was back from her trance, she discovered that her dad was long gone. Sad, she sat down beside him as tears trickled down her cheeks with no word coming out of her mouth.

After some time, she burst out crying, and it came out so uncontrollably, and she was inconsolable. The people that came after hearing her cry could see that she was in so much pain, but they let her cry it all out because they believed that it was the best way to deal with grief and loss.

Her dad was finally buried, and it was time to move on in life, making sure that history remembers his great work. As for herself, not only did she keep his journals and other treasured items from his closet, but she also kept her father's crucifix necklace and THE Hourglass. She passed these on to her son, Alexander, so that he remembers his granddad, and perhaps value the kind of perseverance and determination that the man had.

# CHAPTER SIX
## LUNAR INTERNATIONAL SPACE STATION

D aisy started working on the project of Knight Discoverer as soon as she stopped grieving for her father. She was always hopeful that one of the Space Drones from Carr that had survived the journey through the Black Hole would start sending info about a habitable planet for humankind. Time was at the essence,

After Daisy had been contacted to help build the spaceship, she made good progress in examining the Munerium as has already been alluded to. What was now left for it to do was for it to be used as the technology to build a synthetic Munerium to build the necessary quantity for a spaceship, and that place had to be the moon due to the nature of the oxygen isotope that forms Munerium. This spaceship, Knight Discoverer, was going to be able to withstand the pressure because of intense gravity pull inside the black hole.

So, what was going to contribute to these characteristics, which would allow the synthetic Munerium to not break while inside the black hole? Clearly, some properties that are found in the rocks that are on the moon were supposed to be factored in. People that study Lithology would understand this better, but for the benefits of our wide readers that are not into rocks, Lithology is the study of the general physical features of the rock, or it can simply mean the general characteristics of the rocks.

So, why all the talk about rocks and Lithology? Well, we want to be on the same page as everyone when it comes to the spaceship that Daisy was going to build using her technology. Now, her theory was formulated after observing that the Munerium fell into the desert, and when everyone expected it to break into several pieces, it never did. Therefore, it must obviously have been way too stronger and resistant to force than the natural rocks. In fact, a huge hole was formed where the Munerium had made an impact on the earth.

Later on, in this chapter, we will see why or where did it get its very strong features from. After learning about it, it would be a pleasure to know that these can also be used in making the synthetic version of it, with the full control of humans. So now, instead of just falling from the sky and making people wonder, its synthetic version would be created to come up with a different narrative for its existence. This will now help people make as many discoveries as possible and perhaps create new possibilities for a proper, balanced life elsewhere. This constitutes music to the ears, given what we already spoke about — the amount of damage being caused on Earth because of climate change and anti-climactic human activities that are taking place all over the world.

As such, the composition of chemicals in Munerium, or rather its internal characteristics would be the answer to the building of a resistant spaceship.

So, when we speak about rocks, we know that they exist both on Earth and on the moon. People who study Lithology have good descriptions of the rocks you can find on the moon and earth. In describing these, there is what is called the Oxygen Isotopes that they use to describe these rocks. And, from pasty studies, the rocks on the moon and the ones on earth were said to be identical or had homogeneous features.

But when you look at recent studies, it was found out that oxygen isotopes reveal that earthly and lunar, scientific word for moon, rocks are not as similar as previously thought. So, since these isotopes were not similar, the spaceship that Daisy wanted to build needed to be built on the moon. Why? Well, Daisy did not only want to build it there. But it, being built there, would aid the availability of material containing oxygen isotopes that are strong enough to enable the spaceship to complete its mission.

The history behind the formation of the moon makes it possible that isotopes from there can withstand a lot of pressure. It all begins with Erick J. Cano, Zachary D. Sharp, and Charles K. Shearer, who put up the following statement.

"Our data suggest that samples derived from the deep lunar mantle, which are isotopically heavy compared to Earth, have isotopic compositions that are most representative of the proto-lunar impactor 'Theia.' Our findings imply that the distinct oxygen isotope compositions of Theia and Earth were not completely homogenized by the Moon-forming impact, thus providing quantitative evidence that Theia could have formed farther from the Sun than did Earth."

What stands out from the above is the fact that samples derived from the deep lunar mantle were isotopically heavy compared to Earth. These isotopic compositions were most representative of the proto-lunar impactor 'Theia.' Now, bringing in Theia leads to our next description of how the moon was formed, and we will then wrap this part up by then putting it to you why Daisy's spaceship was supposed to be built on the moon.

So, when it comes to Theia, researchers say that when the moon was formed billions of years ago, in fact, 4.5 billion years ago, it was because of a huge impact that happened between Theia and the Earth. Theia is said to have been as big as Mars in size. Therefore, according to some computer models, the big collision resulted in the formation of the moon. They also say that most of the material that ended up forming the Moon, which is between 70% and 90% of the satellite's composition, came from Theia.

Therefore, given that Theia hit the Earth with such force and was able to keep a lot of its mass and actually formed the moon, we observe that this was one strong object, just like what we learned about Munerium. So, if most of the moon is made up of Theia, then most of the moon has extraordinarily strong characteristics – strong enough to stand against immense pressure. And this same technology could be used to build the spaceship that was being prepared to go and stand against the immense gravitational pull inside the black hole.

As such, one of the main ingredients in synthetic Munerium was the usage of the oxygen isotope found on the moon – we are sure there is plenty of it, given what we just learned about how the moon was formed. Therefore, this was also one other challenge that Daisy was now facing, and, as usual, she intended to win in the end.

All the information that was required, including the tools to be used, was already in place. She had to make sure that the journey to the moon was a success. Perhaps working at NASA was going to come in handy on this matter because where you work sometimes make life hard or easy for you. However, she cared about her work, and nothing was going to stand in her way.

Daisy was working hard on the Knight Discoverer project. She worked so hard her whole life that she never gave herself the luxury of having love affairs, saying that it would only interfere with her work. However, she was really depressed and emotionally frail after her dad's passing. That is when she met a new NASA engineer that had joined her team. He was an experienced engineer that was assigned to Daisy's team to help her in this gigantic project. They became friends, confidants, and lovers. They got married, but Daisy, who was already in her 50's and did not want a child, thought that due to her age, she would not have one. She did not want to have a child in a dying world. But God has plans for all of us that we cannot understand. We just have to say yes to his will.

Daisy was already designing the K.D., and they did not receive any info about the Space Drones released by Carr.

One day she started having morning sickness, and she went to a medical office at NASA, and there she did some blood work. To their surprise, the test finally came out, and Daisy is pregnant.

To her surprise, she said, "I cannot believe this!"

The emotions came running in, and she started crying because of happiness and sadness. She was happy because her family would be going on, but she was also sad because she did not want to have a child in a dying world.

With this mixed emotion in her head, she was walking back to her car when she got a call from her loyal assistant, Marlene.

Daisy answered her phone, saying, "Hi Marlene, you will not believe the news that I have to tell you."

Marlene replied with excitement, "You will not believe the news that I have to tell YOU!"

Daisy, confused, replied, What?????? Tell me.

Marlene said, "You first."

Daisy replied, "No. You go first."

Marlene settled and said, "Are you sitting? This is HUUUUUUUUUUUUUUGE!"

Daisy replied, "I just got to my car. I am sitting. Tell me already!"

Marlene exclaimed, "We found it! We found it!"

Daisy, curious and confused with the conversation, replied, "Found what????????????"

Marlene started crying.

Marlene, filled with excitement and all the emotions all at once, replied, "One of the Space Drones started transmitting DATA from a solar system. This is a dual solar system, and one of the planets is in the habitable zone and has an atmosphere and gases like Earth and with liquid water on its surface! We found Earth 2.0.!"

They both started screaming and crying with happiness, and they could not even contain themselves.

A New Earth, a new beginning for Mankind. Another miracle.

Marlene composed herself and asked Daisy, "What is your news?"

Daisy replied, "I am pregnant. I just came out of the doctor's office. I will have a child"

Marlene started screaming again and exclaimed, "I am so happy for you! Congrats!"

Daisy then replied, "This morning, I had no hope, and now I am full of hope again. Thank you, Lord. You are a Miracle worker."

They name the new Earth Canaan, and the two stars that Canaan orbit were named AFDATA and JSA.

# CHAPTER SEVEN
## FRENEMIES

Here, we would like to take you back to history. We know by now that Daisy's dad passed away after her daughter had broken the good news that his theory would be a success. She had rejoiced together with him while he was by his death bed. And, when he was about to go, he gave his daughter a crucifix so that she would remember him by that. We usually see this happening a lot in our lives, and that should help us to understand what Joseph was doing through that gesture.

Even in the military service that we see in movies, when a soldier is killed on the battlefield, they bring home his or her necklace so that their loved ones would hold on to this for as long as they like. These things hold huge sentimental values, and they are mostly given to people that are the dying favorite person, especially if the dying person is present to award the 'gift' by themselves. So, in this case, Daisy was her dad's favorite.

More so, when these items are passed on, the ones to receive them will also keep them as priced possessions until they identify someone in the family that deserves the recognition. As an example, we see this a lot when someone proposes to their girlfriend, and they say that this ring belonged to my grandmother. If you see a guy with that kind of a ring, know that in most cases, they would be their grandparents or parents' favorites.

As such, Daisy grew up and also had her own son that she loved so much. But not only did the son, named Alexander, behaved well to earn his grandfather's crucifix, but also observed what his mom was doing with her work, and he loved it. Just like his mother when she was young, he also decided that he would become an Astronaut when he grows up. The boy was so serious about this, so much so that he began channeling his energy towards things, or a route that would lead him to Astronomy when he was still very young and when most of his age were spending days fascinating about newly released movies, fashion, and girls. But he was different. He had the maturity of a wise old man and had the work ethic from his mother's bloodline —which turns out to be a huge secret for success in this family.

As he grew up, Alexander was brought up in the Christian tradition. Even though she was a busy lady, his mother always made sure that they observed God, and thus, went to church every weekend. After church, they would usually rest on a good meal discussing life and many other things. It was during these discussions that Alexander would pick up just how amazing him mom was, and how following her route would lead to the creation of an even richer family history. The more he spoke to her over these meals, the more his drive for changing the world grew. At such a rate, there was nothing that was going to stop him.

Luckily for him, we could say he had a mother who had already made history, together with his late granddad. Therefore, many people in this field knew about his Silva family. But still, that did not stop him from working hard even though it was different from the time when Joseph started all this with not many resources or people that believed in him backing his idea up. In fact, Alexander hated it when his mother told him about how people used to ridicule his granddad, saying that his ideas would never be proven because they just would not work. For him, it sounded like it was yesterday, and he felt like it was upon him to work hard and keep on proving people wrong. With such a direction in his thinking, it was easy to pick up Astronomy as a career. But he knew that he had to be careful of friends who pretend to love you, and by night, they go around saying destructive things about you. He was aware of all that and vowed to tread carefully.

For Alexander, it became his drive to do even more so that people respect his family and the inner calling that he always felt to save the world that drove him into doing very well in everything.

He was an incredibly careful and organized boy. Since he was young, and before every important decision, Alexander would hold the crucifix around his neck and say this prayer, "Give me the wisdom and knowledge I need to make this decision. Make me follow your will. Amen."

As he was doing this, he knew in him that he was going to grow up one day and take up responsibility for the lives of many people. This is not something that he took lightly. As such, he would always seek guidance from the Lord. He started doing this when he was still a young boy. And on many occasions, it would not even make sense, but he still would find time to do it repeatedly.

Nevertheless, going back to the enemies of his progress, he knew also that he had to always be watching his back. But he also knew that no matter how hard he watches his back, there would be someone that could sneak bad ideas into his mind or something even worse. As such, he would make sure that he also prays about his safety because he knew that only the power of the Man above would protect him from everything else that seeks to come after his life.

Therefore, this pretty much summed up the life of Alexander as he was growing up under the care of his mother. The two loved each other so much and always took care of each other. During some days even, when he was still young, his mother would come late from work and find him already done with the cooking. If she seemed too hired, he would also offer to do the dishes for her. Between these two, it was always about having each other's back. And this kind of love they took it out of their home into the world, where they did so many wonderful things together with other people, and for the world.

When Alex, as his mother would call him, was about to get out of high school, he gathered a few of his good friends who were good in art and made his mom an unbelievably beautiful portrait of hers. She treasures this so much and always keeps it hung up in her room for everyone to see. Such was the love between them.

# CHAPTER EIGHT
## THE SELECTION

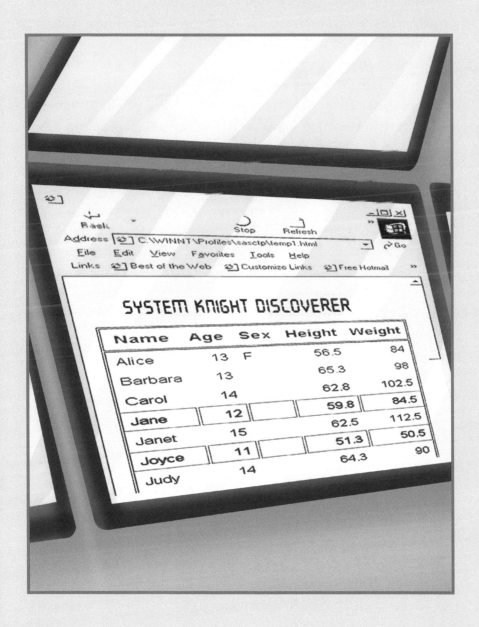

n the year 1960, the world's population was just above 3 billion. And the number kept on rising with time. By the turn of the millennium, the Earth had seen that number more than double to more than 6.1 billion people. During this time, not only was the world's population increasing, by human activity, such as deforestation, was also on the rise because cities kept on growing, and more mines being mined to sustain that growing population.

Therefore, there was a continued rise in population, and as the years went by, it kept on rising exponentially. Coming towards 2070, the Earth was besieged by 10 billion people. And these people continue to feed on the same earth that used to feed only 3 billion people in 1960. That was the birth of all the problems leading to the likes of Joseph and Daisy wanting to go out in space and look for other planets that were suitable for people to live in. Even though these missions were looking impossible to doubters, they were of paramount importance because had they not done that, then the Earth's inhabitants were going to just be stuck on earth with no food to eat and also living under extremely dangerous climatic conditions that kept on changing for the worst.

Now, as life kept on going, and eventually came to 2080, the people of the Earth were dying in their numbers. The reason for their deaths ranged from many natural disasters, as caused by climatic change, to the lack of food because there were just not any more places that they could farm food naturally. Those who could manufactured foods in laboratories, but most of it could not be eaten because it caused cancer in many people, resulting in their painful deaths. So, people were afraid of eating these lab-manufactured foods for fear of death.

Examples of the results of bad climate change include typhoons, excessive droughts, and cyclones. There are many other problems where sometimes, there could excessively rain in one part of the world, resulting in mudslides that kill people in their thousands. Because people were dying and everyone could see it, many people were driven into fear and started fighting for survival by running away to places where it was not entirely easy to live, but at least life could be sustained without having to face too many challenges. But what remained a challenge in these areas is the fact that some powerful people were now the ones with access because, for them, it was easy to just come and drive everyone away. It was now a game of survival.

On the whole planet where 10 Billion inhabitants once lived, there now no more than 1 million people alive in 2132. These ones lived in small settlements around the world that were still livable. All the other places where people once used to live were no more. This was so because of the constrictions of the size of the Earth. When things were normal, we used to hear that the world is made of 25% of land, and the entire 75% is being covered by water. And the water was a composition of liquid water and that of ice —meaning areas where there are extremely low temperatures and the whole land is always ice – or at least most of it – just like in Iceland. So, the areas that are only ice were not there for the sake of existing, but they kept excess water in ice so that the sea levels would not rise and eat up places that are suitable for human settlement.

But, because of climate change, the ice started to melt a long time before the year 2032. that the melting of that ice played a huge role in swallowing up part of the areas where humans used to live before. Now the sea level was high, and people's spaces and those of the animals were being taken up. The lack of space on Earth not only did not make it impossible for humans to live on it, but it also made it possible for the Construction of the Knight Discoverer on the moon. So, this construction would also provide a way for people on Earth to leave behind all these things that they were seeing in their lives because it was scaring them —like their lives were being slowly swallowed up.

The people that were going to be taken into the ship were a limited number. Only 22,000 people could come on board. Two thousand were going to be the crew members from the International Space Command Center composed of scientists, engineers, technicians, military personnel, and the Command Crew, who would take care of 20,000 passengers. These passengers comprised of 10,000 men and women apiece. For the people, this mission was very important because it served as the last hope of mankind surviving extinction. So, no one really wanted to be left behind because who knew, perhaps you were going to be left behind and just die with the rest of the people that remained.

As the people were fighting for a chance to go with the crew into space, it was a sore sight to see. It was clear that everyone wanted to survive, which is OK because people live their lives with this instinct for survival. But here, just reading their eyes could show you that it was more of desperation driving them, way more than ambition. They knew that where they were going could provide a chance for survival. Some families wanted to go in their numbers, but for old people, it was going to be tricky for them to join in because the crew needed people who were going to help them with a lot of work once they settle in the destination. Therefore, those who could not help with the work were naturally left behind.

But, for it to work, and for people to understand, there needed to be a system in place, or a criterion that is agreed upon by many. This way, the crew would be facing fewer challenges in terms of the people complaining about being left behind – or being left to die alone on the fast-shrinking and dying world. So, a process of selection was elaborated to select 20,000 people from the remaining survivors on Earth to come to Knight Discoverer (K.D.). When it was being debated, a point about old people was raised, and some wanted 70 years to be the cut off age. They argued that their relatives, among them who were that age, could still help with chores at home.

As the arguments went on, they discovered that there were far too many young people, and they needed to take them in their numbers so that they could work, and also have a chance to bear more children — in case they managed to go to another livable planet. So, they brought down the maximum allowed age to 60, but still, there was no agreement until they eventually settled for the cut-off age of 50. Therefore, no one above the age of 50 would be selected to go with this mission. These naturally became candidates for facing death in the hands of nature as soon as the Earth was ready to die. It was sad because no one really knew when this day would come. But, at the rate at which livable areas on earth were constricting, the time could be anytime sooner than they anticipated.

As the people that were aged 50 and above were being left, some people felt that it was not fair that people voted for that kind of a decision, especially if it was motivated by the need to provide work. They said many people aged 50 were still feeling and looking young. However, it then emerged that they needed young bloods for more than work or the ability to bear more children. But they needed young people to colonize the new world.

So, as it was decided, all the names of the remaining inhabitants on Earth were placed in a computer system that randomly selected 10,000 males and 10,000 females that would colonize this new world, Canaan.

All the ones selected would stay on Earth until Knight Discoverer was completed and ready for launch in 2135.

# CHAPTER NINE
# LUNAR ROMANCE

As time passed, residents of the Earth were facing a bleak future —something had to be done as soon as possible. As such, Alexander was selected as one of the crew members that would be responsible for managing the Knight Discoverer (KD). This crew would be transported to the moon for training. For them, it was a serious business, and everybody was taking every step seriously. Even in the middle of it all, Alexander's dream was coming true. He cherished science, and he loved using science to save humankind —something he was now lined up to do. It was only going to be a matter of time now, no more turning back!

Therefore, in the year 2133, the crew was lined up to go and complete the training and the final stages of the construction of the KD. Alexander and his people were scheduled to start the testing of all the equipment that was going to help them get to the 'Promised Land.'

Going back to Daisy, Alexander's mom, she was now old at this stage. Even though her age was well advanced now, the people around her and others not in her circles had great respect for her. They respected her because she was the ship designer. Her work of decades was finally going to help people escape problems that were compounding by each day on Earth —her ship would take them to Canaan, the promised land. Because of her works, her son thought it was natural that she was going to be coming with them to the moon for the final stages of the preparations, but he was to receive the shock of his life when he finally brings the subject up before her. Daisy was in her 50's when she gave birth to Alexander, and by now, she thought she was too old to take part in many things.

The Knight Discoverer had been built by the construction crew since 2110. The completion was expected to take 25 years due to the complexity of the project and all technological advances that needed to be implemented and invented to be placed inside such a revolutionary ship. There were just many things, or sciences that were to be included as each stage and every inch of the ship was to be carefully designed and strategically built to withstand the pressure that it would to go through when the time comes.

The ship needed to be very thin and stretched to support the spaghettification process inside the Sagittarius A Star. The amount of pressure that it was going to be going through was immense, hence the need to build it very thin. Alex and his crew understood all this, but instead of them getting anxious about getting things right, they were so excited about seeing their dreams come true. The outmost layer of the spaceship was also built to withstand the spaghettification process. No matter how thin the ship was going to appear, the passengers and crew would still be protected in the inside of the ship, right in the middle of it, so they would not suffer the consequences of the spaghettification process.

So, the crew finally left and found themselves landed on the Lunar Base Station. While here, many good things happened, including Alexander's first feeling of love in a very long time. This love was not the kind that he had for his mother, but the feeling of love for a girl, and indeed, it was a girl that his heart beat fast for. While at it, he was going to have to fight with others because the policy there was that no romantic relationships were to be allowed. But what the heart feels it what it wants.

Sofie was this confident young lady that showed excellence in many things pertaining to their job while on the moon. Besides her beauty, this quality of her also attracted Alexander's attention. She was very competent during their astronaut training sessions and earned Alex's respect. Even if she was good, Alex was excellent, and the two respected each other for that. They then first became friends, confidants, and, before they knew it, they had become lovers.

On the day they first spoke, Sofie was the one that approached Alexander during one of the breaks where people get a chance to talk about things away from work. "I hear your mom designed this." A sweet female voice spoke behind Alexander. He turned around and noticed that, for sure, the sweet voice was in tandem with the looks of the lady that owned it. She was slightly taller than him and had long hair that covered her small head. But even if her head was that small, it perfectly was a match for her big, blue eyes that looked like were borrowed from an angel. Because of her beauty, Alexander was stuck for a while and failed to respond to what she was saying. This did not usually happen to him. He was just a man devoted to his work, and for it to even happen when they were on this important mission was a miracle.

"Ahem," Alexander cleared his throat, trying to say something, but he was clearly stuck, and she jumped into his rescue.

"Sofie," she stretched out her hand to greet him as she said her name.

"Huh?" Alexander replied.

"Sofie, my name is Sofie. They call me Sofia back home, but you can call me Sofie." She smiled at him, and he looked like he was now getting back to the present moment.

"Alright, I see. I know you already. You are the girl trying to take my leading position on the crew. My name is Alexander."

"I know who you are, they all know you. And I am not trying to take anything away from you. I am just good at what I do." She winked at Alexander as she said this. Her beautiful smile seduced him, and he paused for a split second before responding to her. After he did, their conversation turned funny and comfortable for Alexander, leading to their friendship and romance in those months that followed.

Sofie was now in the habit of visiting Alexander in his chambers. On a particular visit, she decided to talk about the pictures that were by Alex's bed. The man was happy to talk about this since he had so much love for his Silva family, both the living and the dead.

"Over there is my family, my science, and my faith." He said

"How do you combine science and faith? Aren't they against one another?" Sofie asked.

"On the contrary. They complement each other. They are part of the same world. What science can't explain; faith helps me understand." Alexander said, before continuing, "I'll show you something."

He got the bible and started reading from the Book of Genesis Chapter 1 from verse 1 all the way to 27. After reading, he looked back at Sofie and said,

"The bible was written thousands of years ago. The book of Genesis is actually talking about the evolution of Our Universe. In the beginning was nothing, and from nothing, everything was created. Light was created. That's the Big Bang. The beginning of everything. The First stars and constellations were created, the first solar systems, Earth was created.

"Like in Genesis, life started in the ocean, and from the ocean, it went on to dry land and animals, from the land, Men and Women were created. You see, the science of evolution and the history in genesis complement each other. Now I ask you, Sofie. How come The Bible that was written thousands of years ago describes so perfectly the evolution of our universe and the life on Earth?" He was looking intently into her eyes. She couldn't stop smiling as she responded.

"I don't know." Sofie replied.

Alexander said, "I don't know either, but my faith tells me that God inspired us to write The Bible and to tell His History. The History of His Creation. The Creation of the Universe and US. He is giving us a second chance to find a new home for the whole humankind."

Alex also pointed out a picture that he had on the wall of his bedroom. It was a picture of a Poem written by a famous 20th Century Astronomer named Carl Sagan. This poem is called "The Pale Blue Dot." Alexander tells Sofie that he loves this poem because it describes how fragile Earth is in the immense emptiness of Space, and how much humans have misbehaved to make this Pale Blue Dot unable to sustain their own lives. Alexander tells Sofie that he hopes that Canaan will be a new chance for a new beginning for Humankind. A place that we should cherish each other and the planet that we live in.

After saying those words, they cuddled into a small hip and drowned in romance. After a while, Sofie discovered that she was pregnant. The two agreed that they could not let anyone know about this because romantic relationships on the Lunar Base station were not allowed altogether. They were to keep this secret until they cross over to the other side – Canaan. The launch of the Space Mission was just about to happen.

# CHAPTER TEN
## THE JOURNEY

The Lunar Base station stay was over since the work that Alexander and his team had gone there to do was done. Their next stop, for the whole crew, was to go back to Earth and enjoy their final moments while there. After a few days' sabbaticals, they would proceed to transport people that were selected in the process to colonize Canaan. These chosen ones were to stay on Earth until the departure date of the Knight Discoverer.

Alexander, still enjoying memories that he created with Sofie on the moon, was seated outside and looking at a Sandstorm forming on the horizon. It took Sofie out of his mind for a moment, even though he imagined how life would be for him and his upcoming baby while in Canaan. On this day, it was the day that the last shuttle was supposed to leave Earth with the last group of selectees. These were to make a stop on the Moon before proceeding with their journey to Canaan.

After some moments, Alex stood up to go and talk to his mother in order to hear how she was feeling about the upcoming trip to the moon, and then to Canaan. In his mind, it was obvious that his mother would want to go there, but to his surprise, he discovered that she was not willing to go anywhere. She reckoned that her days were now numbered. Therefore, there was no need to take a seat that could have been occupied by one younger individual that still had more life ahead of him or her.

Daisy was already old. She had Alex when she was over 50 years old, and by now, she considered herself old for such a mission. When she fell pregnant for Alexander, she was surprised how it happened. She did not want to have a child in a dying world because, according to what her job allowed her to see, the world was dying fast. Therefore, her pregnancy came as a surprise to her. But she kept her child and gave him so much love and hope.

"Hi, mom, time to go to the ship. I hope you are ready and all pumped up for the mission!" He announced himself with overflowing joy. However, his happiness was cut short because he could see that his mother was nowhere near being ready to leave the house. She had not packed anything, especially given the fact that this was the last shuttle to leave —she must have been ready by now, he thought to himself.

"I'm not going anywhere, son." She reluctantly responded, facing downwards as her white hair was the only thing that Alexander could clearly see from his standing position.

"But Mama, THAT'S your ship! You designed and built it! I don't understand?" His face looked worried. His dream of living together with his mom in a better world was going up in smoke right in front of him.

"My work is done, son. I'm not going." This time again, her response was short, and she showed that nothing was going to change her mind. She looked up to her son and continued talking.

"You know, I never told you this. But the same day that I discovered that I was expecting you, one of the missing drones from Carr sent us DATA that it had found a planet that was habitable by humans. It had found Canaan. That gave me hope, and that is why I named you Alexander. Do you know what your name means?"

"I don't. It means I am your son?" They both laughed at his joke. But the laughter was cut short because they knew that they were now going to go their separate ways forever.

As soon as she stopped laughing, she responded to her son. "That too," and with a smile on her face, she said, "But it also means: The Savior of Men. And here you are, the Commander of Knight Discoverer, the last hope of Mankind, the last hope of avoiding our extinction." She continued, showing so much pride for her son. She was, indeed, satisfied with the work that he was doing to complete a mission that started some decades ago.

She continued talking, "Do you think ALL of this is just a coincidence? It is not, son. This is God's Plan. You were born for this mission and for this purpose. Do you believe this?"

He answered, "I do, mother. I will not disappoint you."

Daisy said to Alexander, "I know that you won't. You never did. We can talk about all the theories of the Cosmos, all the mathematics equations to Explain the Universe and Science, but do you know the thing that sums up the whole Universe?" She asked Alex.

Alexander replied, "I don't."

Daisy said, Love, my son. Love is the fundamental force that moves the Universe and everything on it. It connects everything to it. It is more powerful than any force and faster than light. My love for you is infinite and Eternal. It does not matter how far you are or where you are, my LOVE for you will ALWAYS connect us, and God is Love.

Alexander knew her mother very well. If her mind is made up to do something, there was no way that anyone was going to do to change her. He used to thank God that most of her thoughts were for the good of the people. Even if she were to be knuckle-headed about it, people would still benefit and not suffer out of her actions. He knew that she was never going to change her mind. He drew closer to her, she stood up, and the two embraced each other and cried and said their goodbyes. It was not an easy thing for him to give his mother his back for the last time. And for her, it wasn't easy to watch her son's back vanish into the heat of the day. She was seeing him for the last time. Even though she was ready for this day, she still felt like something huge had been plucked out of her life. And for sure, this is what was happening inside her.

By this time, Alexander was a grown man, being 33 years old. Therefore, he knew that he would swallow how his mother had decided to stay and be able to focus on the mission that was in front of him. It was going to take days to recover back to his old, jovial, and determined person. But he hoped that it would take less time because he had an important mission to lead the KD as the ship captain. More so, he felt that the love he had for Sofie was genuine and that she felt the same way about him. As such, he knew she was going to also play an important role in his life – and help him come back to himself.

The time for Alexander and the last crew members to go to the moon finally arrived. Everyone was pumped up and ready to go there. As for Alexander and a few others that had been to the moon once, it was more like business as usual, but for the ordinary people that were selected to go and help with colonizing Canaan, it was their first time being on the moon. They were so ecstatic about the mission. While the likes of Alexander were being worried about their safety, they were busy celebrating what was unfolding in their lives. If they made it to Canaan, it surely would be a double celebration with them.

When the shuttle was ready to embark on the journey, everyone was asked to sit tight and check that all their belts are strapped on strongly. Once everything was set in motion, the shuttle could be seen by distant spectators spewing a blue flame around it. After a few seconds of the flame, it rapidly took off and slowly disappeared into the sky. The last thing that people saw was that small flame turning into a small ball of fire before disappearing, leaving them with smiles and tears of joy that their people were finally going to discover life in a better world.

# CHAPTER ELEVEN
## DECISIONS

The shuttle successfully took the crew and other people from the Earth, and they found themselves on the moon. As soon as they arrived, they did get themselves busy with so many activities to get them ready for the final stretch of their journey – to Canaan. One of the tasks was to emphasize the issue of safety as well as the job that was lying ahead of them. Alexander and the other leaders were busy addressing the people, letting them know what was at stake, as well as assuring them that they would get to Canaan. The people seemed not to understand how such a thin ship was to take them to Canaan, but, as soon as someone from them raised the question, they got satisfactory explanations from Alexander.

"Does anyone have any more questions to ask?" Alexander shouted at the top of his voice. All the people remained silent. It seemed as if they had understood what their leaders were telling them all along. On the other hand, it seemed as if their silence was to confirm that they did not fully understand many things about the ship, and only the crew would know the most. They were right. They only had to worry about their safety —wearing the oxygen helmet properly, to make sure that their gear was rightly on their body to avoid floating in gravity and never coming back down.

Alexander was the Commander of the ship, and Sofie his First Officer. The two were determined to make history together as they prepared to lead the people from the moon station to Canaan. Everybody was strapped up, ready to explore the new planet. "You ready to roll, boy?" Sofie turned towards Alexander as she winked at him. "Oh, yes, we are doing this. And you know what it means, right?"

"What does it mean?" She asked him back as he responded, "It means that we get to raise our baby on the new planet!" He sounded very excited as he lowered his voice so that people around them don't hear about the pregnancy. Sofie responded by giving him the warmest smile he had ever seen. Some of the crew members close by noticed that there was a romance between those two but did not know how far it had stretched.

"But is everything OK with the engines?"

"Yes, relax, we are good to go, and all will be well. I know you want to make your mom proud, and today you are doing this. I am glad to be by your side as you accomplish this."

"But, you are also doing this, Sofie."

"Come on, Alex, you know what I mean. Now, come on in, we got to go." They all made a noise as everyone who was closer to them caught on the celebrations and clapped their hands as they psyched themselves up, getting ready to go. This was going to be the best day for the people on this ship. They were finally getting on the road to escape the problems that the earth was now experiencing.

The K.D, which was made thin to withstand pressure, made a huge noise as it prepared to take off. People inside kept quiet for a while as they looked like scared babies while their bodies were strapped up on the walls of the ship. They held on tight on the side of their spacesuits. Everybody was in silent mode and looked like they were concentrating like soldiers that were at the back of a cargo plane waiting on instructions to take a parachute jump. Finally, the scary take-off was over, and in no time, they found themselves going away from the moon in the famous K.D.

For Alexander, whose last name was Silva after his mother's last name, the journey was important, and even though he had Sofie to keep on talking to, He would sacrifice himself to save the crew and the passengers on board K.D. He had so much responsibility on his shoulders as the Commander of this Space ship, and Sofie was his first Immediate assistant. The two made an exceptionally good team with love and care for the other people.

As they were midway above, Daisy, back on earth, was still not feeling well. Her son was just a few moments in the air with people that he hoped to take to Canaan, the newly discovered planet. She was feeling really weak in her body. Her health was deteriorating fast, and she felt like she was losing her grip on life. Therefore, she asked her caregiver to take her outside the house so that she sees what she called her last sunrise. As she said so, the caregiver thought that she was just messing up with her and insisted that she will be fine. But she, however, took her outside before sunrise.

As this was happening, a minor problem developed on the K.D. The Ionic Engine was reported to be having an issue on the ship's dashboard. Alex immediately got off his seat and headed there to assess the situation. In his heart, he did not want this mission to fail. He got off his seat in haste that everyone noticed that something was wrong. He noticed that this was the same problem that had happened with the failed Allen probe. But Sofie spoke to him that he should calm down so as to keep the people's nerves calm. He took heed and smiled as they calmly walked towards the Ionic Engine room.

As soon as they got to the entrance, they realized that something was not OK, and, using his sharpness, Alex immediately realized that he needed to get there to make a quick fix to it. But he knew that there were dangers involved with such an action. There was a more than 60% chance that he would not come out of there alive. Sofie knew about this too. So, she tried to discourage him from going there. But he turned around to her, and his response was rather heartwarming.

"Sofie, it's OK. It is better for just one person to die than for the rest of the people that are in here."

"I can see that you read the Bible, darling, but this is really happening. I am not ready to lose you."

"And I am not ready to lose myself as I lose you too in the process. Here, hold on to this. I Love you and our unborn child. My love for you is forever. I will always be with you," he concluded as he handed his necklace to Sofie. With shaking hands, she took hold of it with one hand as the other tried to hold Alexander's hand. He quickly looked away as he made way into the Ionic Engine room. Before he entered the room, he said his prayer: Give me the wisdom and knowledge I need to make this decision. Make me follow your will. Amen.

Sofie watched him walk into this room. She thought that if his mother had come with them, she would have been able to stop him. But she did not know that this would not have made a difference because of the love that Alexander had for people as well as the fact that his mother was sick at this moment, and seated outside her house just imagining that his son was somewhere up there trying to save the world.

As soon as she came out of her imagination, Sofie realized that Alex was already there, and there seemed to be excessive light coming from the engine. She shouted for him to stop and come back, but it all fell on deaf ears. As he was stretching his arms wide open and trying to balance himself on top of a beam inside the Ionic Engine, he saw the bracelet that her mom gave to him, which says: GOD'S BLESSINGS AND HARD WORK. Seeing that prompted him to whisper, "This is for you, mom." It surely sounded like his last words as he gathered all the courage that was in him.

Back on Earth, Daisy was still waiting for the sunrise when the burst of light coming from the Ion Engine hit Alexander, vaporizing and killing him in an instant. As it happened, this became the first burst of Sunlight that hit Daisy's eyes, and she opened her arms and screamed out loud, "Alexander!" Her heart beat so fast that it failed in an instant, and she died the same time that her son also vapored into the air. LOVE CONNECTED THEM.

As Alexander sacrificed himself to save the Knight Discoverer, its crew, and passengers, he was vaporized by the Ionic Engine and became dust. His dust was released to the Cosmos through the engine exhaust system. His dust went back to space as stardust once more. It all made sense, after all, humans are believed to be made of stardust as described by some scholars and authors.

In their book, "Living with the Stars: How the Human Body Is Connected to the Life Cycles of the Earth, the Planets, and the Stars," the Astrophysicist Karel Schrijver and his wife Iris Schrijver added their voice to this subject. They said that our bodies are made of the burned-out embers of stars that were released into the galaxy in massive explosions billions of years ago, mixed with atoms that formed only recently as ultrafast rays slammed into Earth's atmosphere.

Therefore, what also happened to Alexander on the ship resembled a 'massive' explosion that burned out his body and exploded it back to the embers of the stars. So, Alexander was released back into space as stardust – the body went back to where it came from in an instant. While watching this happening, Sofie, now joined by one other crew member after hearing her shout to Alexander that he should not go, stood there with her mouth wide open and right hand over her belly. She did not know what to say because her newly found lover had just made a decision to sacrifice his life for those of the people aboard the ship. The fact that Alexander had died left a huge responsibility on her hands because she was now the one to complete the mission as her first in command.

Given that, she needed to pull herself together and continue leading people. Alexander was a courageous man. He would have continued with the mission and then mourned later when everyone else was safe. She thought as she slowly went back to lead the way into Canaan.

Dealing with her grief, Sofie was able to complete the Journey through the Space Jump, and Knight Discoverer was about to enter Sagittarius A Star. This part of the journey would be overly complicated because they were about to enter the black hole.

They enter the Black Hole, and the ship was performing as expected. The Spaghettification process had commenced, and the outmost layer of KD was being compressed and stretched. Meanwhile, the living quarters were well protected.

They did not see anything outside until they entered a region of the Black Hole, called the Inner Event Horizon. After entering this region, a show of light and particles started emerging everywhere. It was like Fireworks from Heaven. It was amazingly beautiful.

They were quickly approaching the Singularity of the Black Hole. A huge flash of light happened, and when the light subsided, they were already on the other side on the Singularity. A New Universe, en route to Canaan. Everyone on the ship celebrated, but Sofie was sad and inconsolable. All the crew tried to cheer her up, but she just had lost the love of her life.

# CHAPTER TWELVE
## CANAAN

After all the bad memories that happened during the journey, especially for Sofie, the ship finally arrived in Canaan. It was a dream come true for all the people in it – perhaps only Sofie was feeling very sad because her unborn child now had no father, who she did not even get a chance to burry. Nevertheless, she had to remain courageous until the mission was completed.

After watching Alexander die, she had gathered her courage and successfully led the rest of the people to Canaan. Because of that, she knew that she could do it again now that people needed leadership again to complete the mission on the soils of Canaan. Sofie did not believe it when the monitor showed the crew that there were finally getting to this new planet that they had never set their foot on. Seeing it there sent the whole crew and some passengers into delirium. They celebrated with high fist pumps as they could feel themselves getting the chance to raise families in a normal place without droughts and so much more.

Landing there was greeted only by sites of beauty. Canaan was a beautiful planet that was 1.5 times bigger than the Earth. The atmosphere there was breathable for humans, and they felt the difference, which really was great news for people running away from polluted air. The planet was exuberant with natural beauties, reminding them of the Earth when it was still in its best days – before human activity destroyed everything that was good about it.

Canaan was covered with Oceans, lakes, and exuberant forests. A paradise given by God for a new beginning for humans. As they looked at this newfound land, they could only hope that they will take better care of this new land.

When the ship finally stopped on the ground, no one among them wanted to be the first to step out. Sofie only opened the doors, and she gestured to the people that they had to wait until some guys among the crew went out, checked it out if everything else was OK. They wanted to make sure that you could breathe normally when they are out there and that the cosmic radiation would not burn you to death before you could even call for help. It was just a matter of precaution, showing how much the crew valued the lives of the people that they were traveling with. They would come back in and signal everyone else to disembark.

Everything was fine. The air was breathable, and there was a small adjustment of the gravity on Canaan that was stronger than Earth's.

So, after discovering the challenge waiting for them, the people decided to pitch tents in a nearby area as they went to sleep. During this first night, not everyone was so sure about what they were doing. Therefore, sleep could not just come easily. Many of them could be heard twisting and turning throughout the night. For the people that could not make love on the moon because of many factors, they saw this as an opportunity to delight themselves with acts of passion together with their loved ones. Who would blame them? They were kind of in a new area that no one really knew what was going to befall them just the following day. So, they wanted to take this opportunity really count.

The following day came, and it gave Sofie's crew a chance to begin a new day in this place. They were happy to see that, for real, the sun also rises the same way it does from where they come from. On the previous day, they landed when the sun had already set, but the outside was clear that they could see things from far. However, they had no chance to explore many things. As such, they now knew about the sunrise in the area, but when it comes to the sun setting, they had no idea how it would be like. Therefore, they were eagerly anticipating this time. It will come, they kept on telling themselves that for the rest of the day.

Finally, the time arrived. For Sofie, this was the first sunset in Canaan, and she experienced it in a special way. While looking at the beautiful Two Star Sunset from JSA and AFDATA stars, she grabbed Alexander's necklace and put her hands over her womb, where her unborn child was quietly sleeping, and she was full of hope again that this time Mankind would learn its lessons and be more gentle and wise with this new home, this new beginning. She thought about this while thinking of the future of her child that she was now carrying.

# BOOK REVIEW

Filho and Alencar's fast-moving tale cites sources ranging from Einstein and Carl Sagan to the book of Genesis (and it seems fair to toss the 2014 movie *Interstellar* in there, too). The language of the narrative is related in a colloquial style more akin to a lecture hall than a brick-thick, hard–SF tome: "But like we mentioned in the previous chapter, these kinds of developments take ample time to bring to completion. No one really wants to produce something that takes that amount of knowledge and time only for it to falter in the end. This is the same thing as what happened in the previous chapter with Joseph and Daisy." While there are some mind-stretching digressions into space-time and quantum entanglement, the simplified plotting and (largely) nontechnical prose make the enjoyable volume suitable for the YA and middle-grade readerships of any planet.

—KIRKUS REVIEWS

CPSIA information can be obtained
at www.ICGtesting.com
Printed in the USA
BVHW020759060421
604307BV00010B/45/J